The Relics of General Chasse

Anthony Trollope

Contents

THE RELICS OF
GENERAL CHASSE

BY

Anthony Trollope

THE RELICS OF GENERAL CHASSE--A TALE OF ANTWERP
by Anthony Trollope

That Belgium is now one of the European kingdoms, living by its own laws, resting on its own bottom, with a king and court, palaces and parliament of its own, is known to all the world. And a very nice little kingdom it is; full of old towns, fine Flemish pictures, and interesting Gothic churches. But in the memory of very many of us who do not think ourselves old men, Belgium, as it is now called--in those days it used to be Flanders and Brabant--was a part of Holland; and it obtained its own independence by a revolution. In that revolution the most important military step was the siege of Antwerp, which was defended on the part of the Dutch by General Chasse, with the utmost gallantry, but nevertheless ineffectually.

After the siege Antwerp became quite a show place; and among the visitors who flocked there to talk of the gallant general, and to see what remained of the great effort which he had made to defend the place, were two Englishmen. One was the hero of this little history; and the other was a young man of considerably less weight in the world. The less I say of the latter the better; but it is necessary that I should give some description of the former.

The Rev. Augustus Horne was, at the time of my narrative, a beneficed clergyman of the Church of England. The profession which he had graced sat easily on him. Its external marks and signs were as pleasing to his friends as were its internal comforts to himself. He was a man of much quiet mirth, full of polished wit, and on some rare occasions he could descend to the more noisy hilarity of a joke. Loved by his friends he loved all the world. He had known no care and seen no sorrow.

Always intended for holy orders he had entered them without a scruple, and remained within their pale without a regret. At twenty-four he had been a deacon, at twenty- seven a priest, at thirty a rector, and at thirty-five a prebendary; and as his rectory was rich and his prebendal stall well paid, the Rev. Augustus Horne was called by all, and called himself, a happy man. His stature was about six feet two, and his corpulence exceeded even those bounds which symmetry would have preferred as being most perfectly compatible even with such a height. But nevertheless Mr. Horne was a well-made man; his hands and feet were small; his face was handsome, frank, and full of expression; his bright eyes twinkled with humour; his finely-cut mouth disclosed two marvellous rows of well-preserved ivory; and his slightly aquiline nose was just such a projection as one would wish to see on the face of a well-fed good-natured dignitary of the Church of England. When I add to all this that the reverend gentleman was as generous as he was rich--and the kind mother in whose arms he had been nurtured had taken care that he should never want--I need hardly say that I was blessed with a very pleasant travelling companion.

I must mention one more interesting particular. Mr. Horne was rather inclined to dandyism, in an innocent way. His clerical starched neckcloth was always of the whitest, his cambric handkerchief of the finest, his bands adorned with the broadest border; his sable suit never degenerated to a rusty brown; it not only gave on all occasions glossy evidence of freshness, but also of the talent which the artisan had displayed in turning out a well-dressed clergyman of the Church of England. His hair was ever brushed with scrupulous attention, and showed in its regular waves the guardian care of each separate bristle. And all this was done with that ease and grace which should be the characteristics of a dignitary of the established English Church.

I had accompanied Mr. Horne to the Rhine; and we had reached Brussels on our return, just at the close of that revolution which ended in affording a throne to the son-in-law of George the Fourth. At that moment General Chasse's name and fame were in every man's mouth, and, like other curious admirers of the brave, Mr. Horne determined to devote two days to the scene of the late events at Antwerp. Antwerp, moreover, possesses perhaps the finest spire, and certainly one of the three or four finest pictures, in the world. Of General Chasse, of the cathedral, and of the Rubens, I had heard much, and was therefore well pleased that such should be his resolution. This accomplished we were to return to Brussels; and thence, via Ghent, Ostend, and Dover, I to complete my legal studies in London, and Mr. Horne to enjoy once more the peaceful retirement of Ollerton rectory. As we were to be absent from Brussels but one night we were enabled to indulge in the gratification of travelling without our luggage. A small sac-de-nuit was prepared; brushes, combs, razors, strops, a change of linen, &c. &c., were carefully put up; but our heavy baggage, our coats, waistcoats, and other wearing apparel were unnecessary. It was delightful to feel oneself so light-handed. The reverend gentleman, with my humble self by his side, left the portal of the Hotel de Belle Vue at 7 a.m., in good humour with all the world. There were no railroads in those days; but a cabriolet, big enough to hold six persons, with rope traces and corresponding appendages, deposited us at the Golden Fleece in something less than six hours. The inward man was duly fortified, and we started for the castle.

It boots not here to describe the effects which gunpowder and grape- shot had had on the walls of Antwerp. Let the curious in these matters read the horrors of the siege of Troy, or the history of Jerusalem taken by Titus. The one may be found in Homer, and the other in Josephus. Or if they prefer doings of a later date there is the taking of Sebastopol, as narrated in the columns of the "Times" newspaper. The accounts are equally true, instructive, and intelligible. In the mean time allow the Rev. Augustus Horne and myself to enter the private chambers of the renowned though defeated general.

We rambled for a while through the covered way, over the glacis and along the counterscarp, and listened to the guide as he detailed to us, in already accustomed words, how the siege had gone. Then we got into the private apartments of the general, and, having dexterously shaken off our attendant, wandered at large among the deserted rooms.

"It is clear that no one ever comes here," said I.

"No," said the Rev. Augustus; "it seems not; and to tell the truth, I don't know why any one should come. The chambers in themselves are not attractive."

What he said was true. They were plain, ugly, square, unfurnished rooms, here a big one, and there a little one, as is usual in most houses;--unfurnished, that is, for the most part. In one place we did find a table and a few chairs, in another a bedstead, and so on. But to me it was pleasant to indulge in those ruminations which any traces of the great or unfortunate create in softly sympathising minds. For a time we communicated our thoughts to each other as we roamed free as air through the apartments; and then I lingered for a few moments behind, while Mr. Horne moved on with a quicker step.

At last I entered the bedchamber of the general, and there I overtook my friend. He was inspecting, with much attention, an article of the great man's wardrobe which he held in his hand. It was precisely that virile habiliment to which a well-known gallant captain alludes in his conversation with the posthumous appearance of Miss Bailey, as containing a Bank of England 5 pound note.

"The general must have been a large man, George, or he would hardly have filled these," said Mr. Horne, holding up to the light the respectable leathern articles in question. "He must have been a very large man,--the largest man in Antwerp, I should think; or else his tailor has done him more than justice."

They were certainly large, and had about them a charming regimental military appearance. They were made of white leather, with bright metal buttons at the knees and bright metal buttons at the top. They owned no pockets, and were, with the exception of the legitimate outlet, continuous in the circumference of the waistband. No dangling strings gave them an appearance of senile imbecility. Were it not for a certain rigidity, sternness, and mental inflexibility,--we will call it military ardour,--with which they were imbued, they would have created envy in the bosom of a fox- hunter.

Mr. Horne was no fox-hunter, but still he seemed to be irresistibly taken with the lady-like propensity of wishing to wear them. "Surely, George," he said, "the general must have been a stouter man than I am"--and he contemplated his own proportions with complacency--"these what's-the-names are quite big enough for me."

I differed in opinion, and was obliged to explain that I thought he did the good living of Ollerton insufficient justice.

"I am sure they are large enough for me," he repeated, with considerable obstinacy. I smiled incredulously; and then to settle the matter he resolved that he would try them on. Nobody had been in these rooms for the last hour, and it appeared as though they were never visited. Even the guide had not come on with us, but was employed in showing other parties about the fortifications. It was clear that this portion of the building was left desolate, and that the experiment might be safely made. So the sportive rector declared that he would for a short time wear the regimentals which had once contained the valorous heart of General Chasse.

With all decorum the Rev. Mr. Horne divested himself of the work of the London artist's needle, and, carefully placing his own garments beyond the reach of dust, essayed to fit himself in military garb.

At that important moment--at the critical instant of the attempt-- the clatter of female voices was heard approaching the chamber. They must have suddenly come round some passage corner, for it was evident by the sound that they were close upon us before we had any warning of their advent. At this very minute Mr. Horne was somewhat embarrassed in his attempts, and was not fully in possession of his usual active powers of movement, nor of his usual presence of mind. He only looked for escape; and seeing a door partly open, he with difficulty retreated through it, and I followed him. We found that we were in a small dressing-room; and as by good luck the door was defended by an inner bolt, my friend was able to protect himself.

"There shall be another siege, at any rate as stout as the last, before I surrender," said he.

As the ladies seemed inclined to linger in the room it became a matter of importance that the above-named articles should fit, not only for ornament but for use. It was very cold, and Mr. Horne was altogether unused to move in a Highland sphere of life. But alas, alas! General Chasse had not been nurtured in the classical retirement of Ollerton. The ungiving leather would stretch no point to accommodate the divine, though it had been willing to minister to the convenience of the soldier. Mr. Horne was vexed and chilled; and throwing the now hateful garments into a corner, and protecting himself from the cold as best he might by standing with his knees together and his body somewhat bent so as to give the skirts of his coat an opportunity of doing extra duty, he begged me to see if those jabbering females were not going to leave him in peace to recover his own property. I accordingly went to the door, and opening it to a small extent I peeped through.

Who shall describe my horror at the sight which I then saw? The scene, which had hitherto been tinted with comic effect, was now becoming so decidedly tragic that I did not dare at once to acquaint my worthy pastor with that which was occurring,--and, alas! had already occurred.

Five country-women of our own--it was easy to know them by their dress and general aspect--were standing in the middle of the room; and one of them, the centre of the group, the senior harpy of the lot, a maiden lady--I could have sworn to that--with a red nose, held in one hand a huge pair of scissors, and in the other--the already devoted goods of my most unfortunate companion! Down from the waistband, through that goodly expanse, a fell gash had already gone through and through; and in useless, unbecoming disorder the broadcloth fell pendant from her arm on this side and on that. At that moment I confess that I had not the courage to speak to Mr. Horne,--not even to look at him.

I must describe that group. Of the figure next to me I could only see the back. It was a broad back done up in black silk not of the newest. The whole figure, one may say, was dumpy. The black silk was not long, as dresses now are worn, nor wide in its skirts. In every way it was skimpy, considering the breadth it had to cover; and below the silk I saw the heels of two thick shoes, and enough to swear by of two woollen stockings. Above the silk was a red and blue shawl; and above that a ponderous, elaborate brown bonnet, as to the materials of which I should not wish to undergo an examination. Over and beyond this I could only see the backs of her two hands. They were held up as though in wonder at that which the red-nosed holder of the scissors had dared to do.

Opposite to this lady, and with her face fully tamed to me, was a kindly-looking, fat motherly woman, with light-coloured hair, not in the best order. She was hot and scarlet with exercise, being perhaps too stout for the steep steps of the fortress; and in one hand she held a handkerchief, with which from time to time she wiped her brow. In the other hand she held one of the extremities of my friend's property, feeling--good, careful soul!--what was the texture of the cloth. As she did so, I could see a glance of approbation pass across her warm features. I liked that lady's face, in spite of her untidy hair, and felt that had she been alone my friend would not have been injured.

On either side of her there stood a flaxen-haired maiden, with long curls, large blue eyes, fresh red cheeks, an undefined lumpy nose, and large good-humoured mouth. They were as like as two peas, only that one was half an inch taller than the other; and there was no difficulty in discovering, at a moment's glance, that they were the children of that over-heated matron who was feeling the web of my friend's cloth.

But the principal figure was she who held the centre place in the group. She was tall and thin, with fierce-looking eyes, rendered more fierce by the spectacles which she wore; with a red nose as I said before; and about her an undescribable something which quite convinced me that she had never known--could never know--aught of the comforts of married life. It was she who held the scissors and the black garments. It was she who had given that unkind cut. As I looked at her she whisked herself quickly round from one companion to the other, triumphing in what she had done, and ready to triumph further in what she was about to do. I immediately conceived a deep hatred for that Queen of the Harpies.

"Well, I suppose they can't be wanted again," said the mother, rubbing her forehead.

"Oh dear no!" said she of the red nose. "They are relics!" I thought to leap forth; but for what purpose should I have leaped? The accursed scissors had already done their work; and the symmetry, nay, even the utility of the vestment was destroyed.

"General Chasse wore a very good article;--I will say that for him," continued the mother.

"Of course he did!" said the Queen Harpy. "Why should he not, seeing that the country paid for it for him? Well, ladies, who's for having a bit?"

"Oh my! you won't go for to cut them up," said the stout back.

"Won't I," said the scissors; and she immediately made another incision. "Who's for having a bit? Don't all speak at once."

"I should like a morsel for a pincushion," said flaxen-haired Miss No. 1, a young lady about nineteen, actuated by a general affection for all sword-bearing, fire-eating heroes. "I should like to have something to make me think of the poor general!"

Snip, snip went the scissors with professional rapidity, and a round piece was extracted from the back of the calf of the left leg. I shuddered with horror; and so did the Rev. Augustus Horne with cold.

"I hardly think it's proper to cut them up," said Miss No. 2.

"Oh isn't it?" said the harpy. "Then I'll do what's improper!" And she got her finger and thumb well through the holes in the scissors' handles. As she spoke resolution was plainly marked on her brow.

"Well, if they are to be cut up, I should certainly like a bit for a pen-wiper," said No. 2. No. 2 was a literary young lady with a periodical correspondence, a journal, and an album. Snip, snip went the scissors again, and the broad part of the upper right division afforded ample materials for a pen-wiper.

Then the lady with the back, seeing that the desecration of the article had been completed, plucked up heart of courage and put in her little request; "I think I might have a needle-case out of it," said she, "just as a suvneer of the poor general"--and a long fragment cut rapidly out of the waistband afforded her unqualified delight.

Mamma, with the hot face and untidy hair, came next. "Well, girls," she said, "as you are all served, I don't see why I'm to be left out. Perhaps, Miss Grogram"-- she was an old maid, you see-- "perhaps, Miss Grogram, you could get me as much as would make a decent-sized reticule."

There was not the slightest difficulty in doing this. The harpy in the centre again went to work, snip, snip, and extracting from that portion of the affairs which usually sustained the greater portion of Mr. Horne's weight two large round pieces of cloth, presented them to the well-pleased matron. "The general knew well where to get a bit of good broadcloth, certainly," said she, again feeling the pieces.

"And now for No. 1," said she whom I so absolutely hated; "I think there is still enough for a pair of slippers. There's nothing so nice for the house as good black cloth slippers that are warm to the feet and don't show the dirt." And so saying, she spread out on the floor the lacerated remainders.

"There's a nice bit there," said young lady No. 2, poking at one of the pockets with the end of her parasol.

"Yes," said the harpy, contemplating her plunder. "But I'm thinking whether I couldn't get leggings as well. I always wear leggings in the thick of the winter." And so she concluded her operations, and there was nothing left but a melancholy skeleton of seams and buttons.

All this having been achieved, they pocketed their plunder and prepared to depart. There are people who have a wonderful appetite for relics. A stone with which Washington had broken a window when a boy--with which he had done so or had not, for there is little difference; a button that was on a coat of Napoleon's, or on that of one of his lackeys; a bullet said to have been picked up at Waterloo or Bunker's Hill; these, and suchlike things are great treasures. And their most desirable characteristic is the ease with which they are attained. Any bullet or any button does the work. Faith alone is necessary. And now these ladies had made themselves happy and glorious with "Relics" of General Chasse cut from the ill-used habiliments of an elderly English gentleman!

They departed at last, and Mr. Horne, for once in an ill humour, followed me into the bedroom. Here I must be excused if I draw a veil over his manly sorrow at discovering what fate had done for him. Remember what was his position, unclothed in the Castle of Antwerp! The nearest suitable change for those which had been destroyed was locked up in his portmanteau at the Hotel de Belle Rue in Brussels! He had nothing left to him--literally nothing, in that Antwerp world. There was no other wretched being wandering then in that Dutch town so utterly denuded of the goods of life. For what is a man fit,--for what can he be fit,--when left in such a position? There are some evils which seem utterly to crush a man; and if there be any misfortune to which a man may be allowed to succumb without imputation on his manliness, surely it is such as this. How was Mr. Horne to return to his hotel without incurring the displeasure of the municipality? That was my first thought.

He had a cloak, but it was at the inn; and I found that my friend was oppressed with a great horror at the idea of being left alone; so that I could not go in search of it. There is an old saying, that no man is a hero to his valet de chambre, the reason doubtless being this, that it is customary for his valet to see the hero divested of those trappings in which so much of the heroic consists. Who reverences a clergyman without his gown, or a warrior without his sword and sabre-tasche? What would even Minerva be without her helmet?

I do not wish it to be understood that I no longer reverenced Mr. Horne because he was in an undress; but he himself certainly lost much of his composed, well-sustained dignity of demeanour. He was fearful and querulous, cold, and rather cross. When, forgetting his size, I offered him my own, he thought that I was laughing at him. He began to be afraid that the story would get abroad, and he then and there exacted a promise that I would never tell it during his lifetime. I have kept my word; but now my old friend has been gathered to his fathers, full of years.

At last I got him to the hotel. It was long before he would leave the castle, cloaked though he was;--not, indeed, till the shades of evening had dimmed the outlines of men and things, and made indistinct the outward garniture of those who passed to and fro in the streets. Then, wrapped in his cloak, Mr. Horne followed me along the quays and through the narrowest of the streets; and at length, without venturing to return the gaze of any one in the hotel court, he made his way up to his own bedroom.

Dinnerless and supperless he went to his couch. But when there he did consent to receive some consolation in the shape of mutton cutlets and fried potatoes, a savory omelet, and a bottle of claret. The mutton cutlets and fried potatoes at the Golden Fleece at Antwerp are--or were then, for I am speaking now of well-nigh thirty years since--remarkably good; the claret, also, was of the best; and so, by degrees, the look of despairing dismay passed from his face, and some scintillations of the old fire returned to his eyes.

"I wonder whether they find themselves much happier for what they have got?" said he.

"A great deal happier," said I. "They'll boast of those things to all their friends at home, and we shall doubtless see some account of their success in the newspapers."

"It would be delightful to expose their blunder,--to show them up. Would it not, George? To turn the tables on them?"

"Yes," said I, "I should like to have the laugh against them."

"So would I, only that I should compromise myself by telling the story. It wouldn't do at all to have it told at Oxford with my name attached to it."

To this also I assented. To what would I not have assented in my anxiety to make him happy after his misery?

But all was not over yet. He was in bed now, but it was necessary that he should rise again on the morrow. At home, in England, what was required might perhaps have been made during the night; but here, among the slow Flemings, any such exertion would have been impossible. Mr. Horne, moreover, had no desire to be troubled in his retirement by a tailor.

Now the landlord of the Golden Fleece was a very stout man,--a very stout man indeed. Looking at him as he stood with his hands in his pockets at the portal of his own establishment, I could not but think that he was stouter even than Mr. Horne. But then he was certainly much shorter, and the want of due proportion probably added to his unwieldy appearance. I walked round him once or twice wishfully, measuring him in my eye, and thinking of what texture might be the Sunday best of such a man. The clothes which he then had on were certainly not exactly suited to Mr. Horne's tastes.

He saw that I was observing him, and appeared uneasy and offended. I had already ascertained that he spoke a little English. Of Flemish I knew literally nothing, and in French, with which probably he was also acquainted, I was by no means voluble. The business which I had to transact was intricate, and I required the use of my mother-tongue.

It was intricate and delicate, and difficult withal. I began by remarking on the weather, but he did not take my remarks kindly. I am inclined to fancy that he thought I was desirous of borrowing money from him. At any rate he gave me no encouragement in my first advances.

"Vat misfortune?" at last he asked, when I had succeeded in making him understand that a gentleman up stairs required his assistance.

"He has lost these things," and I took hold of my own garments. "It's a long story, or I'd tell you how; but he has not a pair in the world till he gets back to Brussels,--unless you can lend him one."

"Lost hees br-?" and he opened his eyes wide, and looked at me with astonishment.

"Yes, yes, exactly so," said I, interrupting him. "Most astonishing thing, isn't it? But it's quite true."

"Vas hees money in de pocket?" asked my auspicious landlord.

"No, no, no. It's not so bad as that, his money is all right. I had the money, luckily."

"Ah! dat is better. But he have lost hees b-?"

"Yes, yes;" I was now getting rather impatient. "There is no mistake about it. He has lost them as sure as you stand there." And then I proceeded to explain that as the gentleman in question was very stout, and as he, the landlord, was stoat also, he might assist us in this great calamity by a loan from his own wardrobe.

When he found that the money was not in the pocket, and that his bill therefore would be paid, he was not indisposed to be gracious. He would, he said, desire his servant to take up what was required to Mr. Horne's chamber. I endeavoured to make him understand that a sombre colour would be preferable; but he only answered that he would put the best that he had at the gentleman's disposal. He could not think of offering anything less than his best on such an occasion. And then he turned his back and went his way, muttering as he went something in Flemish, which I believed to be an exclamation of astonishment that any man should, under any circumstances, lose such an article.

It was now getting late; so when I had taken a short stroll by myself, I went to bed without disturbing Mr. Horne again that night. On the following morning I thought it best not to go to him unless he sent for me; so I desired the boots to let him know that I had ordered breakfast in a private room, and that I would await him there unless he wished to see me. He sent me word back to say that he would be with me very shortly.

He did not keep me waiting above half an hour, but I confess that that half hour was not pleasantly spent. I feared that his temper would be tried in dressing, and that he would not be able to eat his breakfast in a happy state of mind. So that when I heard his heavy footstep advancing along the passage my heart did misgive me, and I felt that I was trembling.

That step was certainly slower and more ponderous than usual. There was always a certain dignity in the very sound of his movements, but now this seemed to have been enhanced. To judge merely by the step one would have said that a bishop was coming that way instead of a prebendary.

And then he entered. In the upper half of his august person no alteration was perceptible. The hair was as regular and as graceful as ever, the handkerchief as white, the coat as immaculate; but below his well-filled waistcoat a pair of red plush began to shine in unmitigated splendour, and continued from thence down to within an inch above his knee; nor, as it appeared, could any pulling induce them to descend lower. Mr. Horne always wore black silk stockings,--at least so the world supposed, but it was now apparent that the world had been wrong in presuming him to be guilty of such extravagance. Those, at any rate, which he exhibited on the present occasion were more economical. They were silk to the calf, but thence upwards they continued their career in white cotton. These then followed the plush; first two snowy, full-sized pillars of white, and then two jet columns of flossy silk. Such was the appearance, on that well-remembered morning, of the Rev. Augustus Horne, as he entered the room in which his breakfast was prepared.

I could see at a glance that a dark frown contracted his eyebrows, and that the compressed muscles of his upper lip gave a strange degree of austerity to his open face. He carried his head proudly on high, determined to be dignified in spite of his misfortunes, and advanced two steps into the room without a remark, as though he were able to show that neither red plush nor black cloth could disarrange the equal poise of his mighty mind!

And after all what are a man's garments but the outward husks in which the fruit is kept, duly tempered from the wind?

"The rank is but the guinea stamp, The man's the gowd for a' that."

And is not the tailor's art as little worthy, as insignificant as that of the king who makes

"A marquis, duke, and a' that"?

Who would be content to think that his manly dignity depended on his coat and waistcoat, or his hold on the world's esteem on any other garment of usual wear? That no such weakness soiled his mind Mr. Horne was determined to prove; and thus he entered the room with measured tread, and stern dignified demeanour.

Having advanced two steps his eye caught mine. I do not know whether he was moved by some unconscious smile on my part;--for in truth I endeavoured to seem as indifferent as himself to the nature of his dress;--or whether he was invincibly tickled by some inward fancy of his own, but suddenly his advancing step ceased, a broad flash of comic humour spread itself over his features, he retreated with his back against the wall, and then burst out into an immoderate roar of loud laughter.

And I--what else could I then do but laugh? He laughed, and I laughed. He roared, and I roared. He lifted up his vast legs to view till the rays of the morning sun shone through the window on the bright hues which he displayed; and he did not sit down to his breakfast till he had in every fantastic attitude shown off to the best advantage the red plush of which he had so recently become proud.

An Antwerp private cabriolet on that day reached the yard of the Hotel de

Belle Vue at about 4 p.m., and four waiters, in a frenzy of astonishment, saw the Reverend Augustus Horne descend from the vehicle and seek his chamber dressed in the garments which I have described. But I am inclined to think that he never again favoured any of his friends with such a sight.

It was on the next evening after this that I went out to drink tea with two maiden ladies, relatives of mine, who kept a seminary for English girls at Brussels. The Misses Macmanus were very worthy women, and earned their bread in an upright, painstaking manner. I would not for worlds have passed through Brussels without paying them this compliment. They were, however, perhaps a little dull, and I was aware that I should not probably meet in their drawing- room many of the fashionable inhabitants of the city. Mr. Horne had declined to accompany me; but in doing so he was good enough to express a warm admiration for the character of my worthy cousins.

The elder Miss Macmanus, in her little note, had informed me that she would have the pleasure of introducing me to a few of my "compatriots." I presumed she meant Englishmen; and as I was in the habit of meeting such every day of my life at home, I cannot say that I was peculiarly elevated by the promise. When, however, I entered the room, there was no Englishman there;--there was no man of any kind. There were twelve ladies collected together with the view of making the evening pass agreeably to me, the single virile being among them all. I felt as though I were a sort of Mohammed in Paradise; but I certainly felt also that the Paradise was none of my own choosing.

In the centre of the amphitheatre which the ladies formed sat the two Misses Macmanus;--there, at least, they sat when they had completed the process of shaking hands with me. To the left of them, making one wing of the semicircle, were arranged the five pupils by attending to whom the Misses Macmanus earned their living; and the other wing consisted of the five ladies who had furnished themselves with relics of General Chasse. They were my "compatriots."

I was introduced to them all, one after the other; but their names did not abide in my memory one moment. I was thinking too much of the singularity of the adventure, and could not attend to such minutiae. That the red-rosed harpy was Miss Grogram, that I remembered;--that, I may say, I shall never forget. But whether the motherly lady with the somewhat blowsy hair was Mrs. Jones, or Mrs. Green, or

Mrs. Walker, I cannot now say. The dumpy female with the broad back was always called Aunt Sally by the young ladies.

Too much sugar spoils one's tea; I think I have heard that even prosperity will cloy when it comes in overdoses; and a schoolboy has been known to be overdone with jam. I myself have always been peculiarly attached to ladies' society, and have avoided bachelor parties as things execrable in their very nature. But on this special occasion I felt myself to be that schoolboy;--I was literally overdone with jam. My tea was all sugar, so that I could not drink it. I was one among twelve. What could I do or say? The proportion of alloy was too small to have any effect in changing the nature of the virgin silver, and the conversation became absolutely feminine.

I must confess also that my previous experience as to these compatriots of mine had not prejudiced me in their favour. I regarded them with,--I am ashamed to say so, seeing that they were ladies,--but almost with loathing. When last I had seen them their occupation had reminded me of some obscene feast of harpies, or almost of ghouls. They had brought down to the verge of desperation the man whom of all men I most venerated. On these accounts I was inclined to be taciturn with reference to them;--and then what could I have to say to the Misses Macmanus's five pupils?

My cousin at first made an effort or two in my favour, but these efforts were fruitless. I soon died away into utter unrecognised insignificance, and the conversation, as I have before said, became feminine. And indeed that horrid Miss Grogram, who was, as it were, the princess of the ghouls, nearly monopolised the whole of it. Mamma Jones--we will call her Jones for the occasion--put in a word now and then, as did also the elder and more energetic Miss Macmanus. The dumpy lady with the broad back ate tea-cake incessantly; the two daughters looked scornful, as though they were above their company with reference to the five pupils; and the five pupils themselves sat in a row with the utmost propriety, each with her hands crossed on her lap before her.

Of what they were talking at last I became utterly oblivious. They had ignored me, going into realms of muslin, questions of maid- servants, female rights, and cheap under-clothing; and I therefore had ignored them. My mind had gone back to Mr. Horne and his garments. While they spoke of their rights, I was thinking of his wrongs; when they mentioned the price of flannel, I thought of that of broadcloth.

But of a sudden my attention was arrested. Miss Macmanus had said something of the black silks of Antwerp, when Miss Grogram replied that she had just returned from that city and had there enjoyed a great success. My cousin had again asked something about the black silks, thinking, no doubt, that Miss Grogram had achieved some bargain, but that lady had soon undeceived her.

"Oh no," said Miss Grogram, "it was at the castle. We got such beautiful relics of General Chasse! Didn't we, Mrs. Jones?"

"Indeed we did," said Mrs. Jones, bringing out from beneath the skirts of her dress and ostensibly displaying a large black bag.

"And I've got such a beautiful needle-case," said the broad-back, displaying her prize. "I've been making it up all the morning." And she handed over the article to Miss Macmanus.

"And only look at this duck of a pen-wiper," simpered flaxen-hair No. 2. "Only think of wiping one's pens with relics of General Chasse!" and she handed it over to the other Miss Macmanus.

"And mine's a pin-cushion," said No. 1, exhibiting the trophy.

"But that's nothing to what I've got," said Miss Grogram. "In the first place, there's a pair of slippers,--a beautiful pair;--they're not made up yet, of course; and then--"

The two Misses Macmanus and their five pupils were sitting open- eared, open-eyed, and open-mouthed. How all these sombre-looking articles could be relics of General Chasse did not at first appear clear to them.

"What are they, Miss Grogram?" said the elder Miss Macmanus, holding the needle-case in one hand and Mrs. Jones's bag in the other. Miss Macmanus was a strong-minded female, and I reverenced my cousin when I saw the decided way in which she intended to put down the greedy arrogance of Miss Grogram.

"They are relics."

"But where do they come from, Miss Grogram?"

"Why, from the castle, to be sure;--from General Chasse's own rooms."

"Did anybody sell them to you?"

"No."

"Or give them to you?"

"Why, no;--at least not exactly give."

"There they were, and she took 'em," said the broad-back. Oh, what a look Miss Grogram gave her! "Took them! of course I took them. That is, you took them as much as I did. They were things that we found lying about."

"What things?" asked Miss Macmanus, in a peculiarly strong-minded tone.

Miss Grogram seemed to be for a moment silenced. I had been ignored, as I have said, and my existence forgotten; but now I observed that the eyes of the culprits were turned towards me,--the eyes, that is, of four of them. Mrs. Jones looked at me from beneath her fan; the two girls glanced at me furtively, and then their eyes fell to the lowest flounces of their frocks.

Miss Grogram turned her spectacles right upon me, and I fancied that she nodded her head at me as a sort of answer to Miss Macmanus. The five pupils opened their mouths and eyes wider; but she of the broad back was nothing abashed. It would have been nothing to her had there been a dozen gentlemen in the room. "We just found a pair of black--." The whole truth was told in the plainest possible language.

"Oh, Aunt Sally!" "Aunt Sally, how can you?" "Hold your tongue, Aunt Sally!"

"And then Miss Grogram just cut them up with her scissors," continued Aunt Sally, not a whit abashed, "and gave us each a bit, only she took more than half for herself." It was clear to me that there had been some quarrel, some delicious quarrel, between Aunt Sally and Miss Grogram. Through the whole adventure I had rather respected Aunt Sally. "She took more than half for herself," continued Aunt Sally. "She kept all the--"

"Jemima," said the elder Miss Macmanus, interrupting the speaker and addressing her sister, "it is time, I think, for the young ladies to retire. Will you be kind enough to see them to their rooms?" The five pupils thereupon rose from their seats--and courtesied. They then left the room in file, the younger Miss Macmanus showing them the way.

"But we haven't done any harm, have we?" asked Mrs. Jones, with some tremulousness in her voice.

"Well, I don't know," said Miss Macmanus. "What I'm thinking of now is this;--to whom, I wonder, did the garments properly belong? Who had been the owner and wearer of them?"

"Why, General Chasse of course," said Miss Grogram.

"They were the general's," repeated the two young ladies; blushing, however, as they alluded to the subject.

"Well, we thought they were the general's, certainly; and a very excellent article they were," said Mrs. Jones.

"Perhaps they were the butler's?" said Aunt Sally. I certainly had not given her credit for so much sarcasm.

"Butler's!" exclaimed Miss Grogram, with a toss of her head.

"Oh, Aunt Sally, Aunt Sally! how can you?" shrieked the two young ladies.

"Oh laws!" ejaculated Mrs. Jones.

"I don't think that they could have belonged to the butler," said Miss Macmanus, with much authority, "seeing that domestics in this country are never clad in garments of that description; so far my own observation enables me to speak with certainty. But it is equally sure that they were never the property of the general lately in command at Antwerp. Generals, when they are in full dress, wear ornamental lace upon their--their regimentals; and when--" So much she said, and something more, which it may be unnecessary that I should repeat; but such were her eloquence and logic that no doubt would have been left on the mind of any impartial hearer. If an argumentative speaker ever proved anything, Miss Macmanus proved that General Chasse had never been the wearer of the article in question.

"But I know very well they were his!" said Miss Grogram, who was not an impartial hearer. "Of course they were; whose else's should they be?"

"I'm sure I hope they were his," said one of the young ladies, almost crying.

"I wish I'd never taken it," said the other.

"Dear, dear, dear!" said Mrs. Jones.

"I'll give you my needle-case, Miss Grogram," said Aunt Sally.

I had sat hitherto silent during the whole scene, meditating how best I might confound the red-nosed harpy. Now, I thought, was the time for me to strike in.

"I really think, ladies, that there has been some mistake," said I.

"There has been no mistake at all, sir!" said Miss Grogram.

"Perhaps not," I answered, very mildly; "very likely not. But some affair of a similar nature was very much talked about in Antwerp yesterday."

"Oh laws!" again ejaculated Mrs. Jones.

"The affair I allude to has been talked about a good deal, certainly," I continued. "But perhaps it may be altogether a different circumstance."

"And what may be the circumstance to which you allude?" asked Miss Macmanus, in the same authoritative tone.

"I dare say it has nothing to do with these ladies," said I; "but an article of dress, of the nature they have described, was cut up in the Castle of Antwerp on the day before yesterday. It belonged to a gentleman who was visiting the place; and I was given to understand that he is determined to punish the people who have wronged him."

"It can't be the same," said Miss Grogram; but I could see that she was trembling.

"Oh laws! what will become of us?" said Mrs. Jones.

"You can all prove that I didn't touch them, and that I warned her not," said Aunt Sally. In the mean time the two young ladies had almost fainted behind their fans.

"But how had it come to pass," asked Miss Macmanus, "that the gentleman had--"

"I know nothing more about it, cousin," said I; "only it does seem that there is an odd coincidence."

Immediately after this I took my leave. I saw that I had avenged my friend, and spread dismay in the hearts of these who had injured him. I had learned in the course of the evening at what hotel the five ladies were staying; and in the course of the next morning I sauntered into the hall, and finding one of the porters alone, asked if they were still there. The man told me that they had started by the earliest diligence. "And," said he, "if you are a friend of theirs, perhaps you will take charge of these things, which they have left behind them?" So saying, he pointed to a table at the back of the hall, on which were lying the black bag, the black needle-case, the black pin cushion, and the black pen-wiper. There was also a heap of fragments of cloth which I well knew had been intended by Miss Grogram for the comfort of her feet and ancles.

I declined the commission, however. "They were no special friends of mine," I said; and I left all the relics still lying on the little table in the back hall.

"Upon the whole, I am satisfied!" said the Rev. Augustus Horne, when I told him the finale of the story.

The Codes Of Hammurabi And Moses
W. W. Davies

QTY

The discovery of the Hammurabi Code is one of the greatest achievements of archaeology, and is of paramount interest, not only to the student of the Bible, but also to all those interested in ancient history...

Religion   **ISBN:** *1-59462-338-4*   **Pages:132**

MSRP $12.95

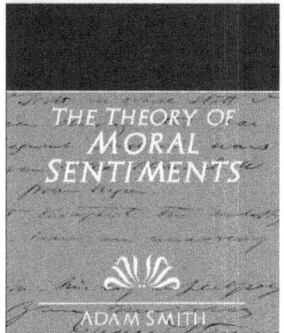

The Theory of Moral Sentiments
Adam Smith

QTY

This work from 1749. contains original theories of conscience amd moral judgment and it is the foundation for systemof morals.

Philosophy   ISBN: *1-59462-777-0*   **Pages:536**

MSRP $19.95

Jessica's First Prayer
Hesba Stretton

QTY

In a screened and secluded corner of one of the many railway-bridges which span the streets of London there could be seen a few years ago, from five o'clock every morning until half past eight, a tidily set-out coffee-stall, consisting of a trestle and board, upon which stood two large tin cans, with a small fire of charcoal burning under each so as to keep the coffee boiling during the early hours of the morning when the work-people were thronging into the city on their way to their daily toil...

Pages:84

Childrens   ISBN: *1-59462-373-2*   *MSRP $9.95*

My Life and Work
Henry Ford

QTY

Henry Ford revolutionized the world with his implementation of mass production for the Model T automobile. Gain valuable business insight into his life and work with his own auto-biography... "We have only started on our development of our country we have not as yet, with all our talk of wonderful progress, done more than scratch the surface. The progress has been wonderful enough but..."

Pages:300

Biographies/   ISBN: *1-59462-198-5*   *MSRP $21.95*

The Art of Cross-Examination
Francis Wellman

QTY

I presume it is the experience of every author, after his first book is published upon an important subject, to be almost overwhelmed with a wealth of ideas and illustrations which could readily have been included in his book, and which to his own mind, at least, seem to make a second edition inevitable. Such certainly was the case with me; and when the first edition had reached its sixth impression in five months, I rejoiced to learn that it seemed to my publishers that the book had met with a sufficiently favorable reception to justify a second and considerably enlarged edition. ..

Pages:412

Reference   ISBN: *1-59462-647-2*   *MSRP $19.95*

On the Duty of Civil Disobedience
Henry David Thoreau

QTY

Thoreau wrote his famous essay, On the Duty of Civil Disobedience, as a protest against an unjust but popular war and the immoral but popular institution of slave-owning. He did more than write—he declined to pay his taxes, and was hauled off to gaol in consequence. Who can say how much this refusal of his hastened the end of the war and of slavery ?

Law   ISBN: *1-59462-747-9*   **Pages:48**

MSRP $7.45

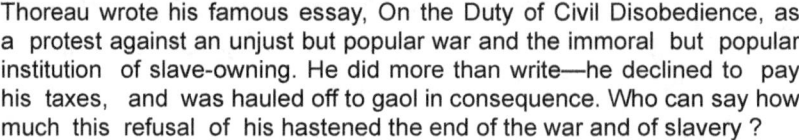

Dream Psychology Psychoanalysis for Beginners
Sigmund Freud

QTY

Sigmund Freud, born Sigismund Schlomo Freud (May 6, 1856 - September 23, 1939), was a Jewish-Austrian neurologist and psychiatrist who co-founded the psychoanalytic school of psychology. Freud is best known for his theories of the unconscious mind, especially involving the mechanism of repression; his redefinition of sexual desire as mobile and directed towards a wide variety of objects; and his therapeutic techniques, especially his understanding of transference in the therapeutic relationship and the presumed value of dreams as sources of insight into unconscious desires.

Pages:196

Psychology   ISBN: *1-59462-905-6*   *MSRP $15.45*

The Miracle of Right Thought
Orison Swett Marden

QTY

Believe with all of your heart that you will do what you were made to do. When the mind has once formed the habit of holding cheerful, happy, prosperous pictures, it will not be easy to form the opposite habit. It does not matter how improbable or how far away this realization may see, or how dark the prospects may be, if we visualize them as best we can, as vividly as possible, hold tenaciously to them and vigorously struggle to attain them, they will gradually become actualized, realized in the life. But a desire, a longing without endeavor, a yearning abandoned or held indifferently will vanish without realization.

Pages:360

Self Help   ISBN: *1-59462-644-8*   *MSRP $25.45*

QTY

☐ **The Rosicrucian Cosmo-Conception Mystic Christianity** *by Max Heindel*   ISBN: *1-59462-188-8*   **$38.95**
The Rosicrucian Cosmo-conception is not dogmatic, neither does it appeal to any other authority than the reason of the student. It is: not controversial, but is: sent forth in the, hope that it may help to clear...   New Age/Religion Pages 646

☐ **Abandonment To Divine Providence** *by Jean-Pierre de Caussade*   ISBN: *1-59462-228-0*   **$25.95**
"The Rev. Jean Pierre de Caussade was one of the most remarkable spiritual writers of the Society of Jesus in France in the 18th Century. His death took place at Toulouse in 1751. His works have gone through many editions and have been republished...   Inspirational/Religion Pages 400

☐ **Mental Chemistry** *by Charles Haanel*   ISBN: *1-59462-192-6*   **$23.95**
Mental Chemistry allows the change of material conditions by combining and appropriately utilizing the power of the mind. Much like applied chemistry creates something new and unique out of careful combinations of chemicals the mastery of mental chemistry...   New Age Pages 354

☐ **The Letters of Robert Browning and Elizabeth Barret Barrett 1845-1846 vol II**   ISBN: *1-59462-193-4*   **$35.95**
by Robert Browning and Elizabeth Barrett   Biographies Pages 596

☐ **Gleanings In Genesis (volume I)** *by Arthur W. Pink*   ISBN: *1-59462-130-6*   **$27.45**
Appropriately has Genesis been termed "the seed plot of the Bible" for in it we have, in germ form, almost all of the great doctrines which are afterwards fully developed in the books of Scripture which follow...   Religion/Inspirational Pages 420

☐ **The Master Key** *by L. W. de Laurence*   ISBN: *1-59462-001-6*   **$30.95**
In no branch of human knowledge has there been a more lively increase of the spirit of research during the past few years than in the study of Psychology, Concentration and Mental Discipline. The requests for authentic lessons in Thought Control, Mental Discipline and...   New Age/Business Pages 422

☐ **The Lesser Key Of Solomon Goetia** *by L. W. de Laurence*   ISBN: *1-59462-092-X*   **$9.95**
This translation of the first book of the "Lernegton" which is now for the first time made accessible to students of Talismanic Magic was done, after careful collation and edition, from numerous Ancient Manuscripts in Hebrew, Latin, and French...   New Age/Occult Pages 92

☐ **Rubaiyat Of Omar Khayyam** *by Edward Fitzgerald*   ISBN: *1-59462-332-5*   **$13.95**
Edward Fitzgerald, whom the world has already learned, in spite of his own efforts to remain within the shadow of anonymity, to look upon as one of the rarest poets of the century, was born at Bredfield, in Suffolk, on the 31st of March, 1809. He was the third son of John Purcell...   Music Pages 172

☐ **Ancient Law** *by Henry Maine*   ISBN: *1-59462-128-4*   **$29.95**
The chief object of the following pages is to indicate some of the earliest ideas of mankind, as they are reflected in Ancient Law, and to point out the relation of those ideas to modern thought.   Religiom/History Pages 452

☐ **Far-Away Stories** *by William J. Locke*   ISBN: *1-59462-129-2*   **$19.45**
"Good wine needs no bush, but a collection of mixed vintages does. And this book is just such a collection. Some of the stories I do not want to remain buried for ever in the museum files of dead magazine-numbers an author's not unpardonable vanity..."   Fiction Pages 272

☐ **Life of David Crockett** *by David Crockett*   ISBN: *1-59462-250-7*   **$27.45**
"Colonel David Crockett was one of the most remarkable men of the times in which he lived. Born in humble life, but gifted with a strong will, an indomitable courage, and unremitting perseverance...   Biographies/New Age Pages 424

☐ **Lip-Reading** *by Edward Nitchie*   ISBN: *1-59462-206-X*   **$25.95**
Edward B. Nitchie, founder of the New York School for the Hard of Hearing, now the Nitchie School of Lip-Reading, Inc, wrote "LIP-READING Principles and Practice". The development and perfecting of this meritorious work on lip-reading was an undertaking...   How-to Pages 400

☐ **A Handbook of Suggestive Therapeutics, Applied Hypnotism, Psychic Science**   ISBN: *1-59462-214-0*   **$24.95**
by Henry Munro   Health/New Age/Health/Self-help Pages 376

☐ **A Doll's House: and Two Other Plays** *by Henrik Ibsen*   ISBN: *1-59462-112-8*   **$19.95**
Henrik Ibsen created this classic when in revolutionary 1848 Rome. Introducing some striking concepts in playwriting for the realist genre, this play has been studied the world over.   Fiction/Classics/Plays 308

☐ **The Light of Asia** *by sir Edwin Arnold*   ISBN: *1-59462-204-3*   **$13.95**
In this poetic masterpiece, Edwin Arnold describes the life and teachings of Buddha. The man who was to become known as Buddha to the world was born as Prince Gautama of India but he rejected the worldly riches and abandoned the reigns of power when...   Religion/History/Biographies Pages 170

☐ **The Complete Works of Guy de Maupassant** *by Guy de Maupassant*   ISBN: *1-59462-157-8*   **$16.95**
"For days and days, nights and nights, I had dreamed of that first kiss which was to consecrate our engagement, and I knew not on what spot I should put my lips..."   Fiction/Classics Pages 240

☐ **The Art of Cross-Examination** *by Francis L. Wellman*   ISBN: *1-59462-309-0*   **$26.95**
Written by a renowned trial lawyer, Wellman imparts his experience and uses case studies to explain how to use psychology to extract desired information through questioning.   How-to/Science/Reference Pages 408

☐ **Answered or Unanswered?** *by Louisa Vaughan*   ISBN: *1-59462-248-5*   **$10.95**
Miracles of Faith in China   Religion Pages 112

☐ **The Edinburgh Lectures on Mental Science (1909)** *by Thomas*   ISBN: *1-59462-008-3*   **$11.95**
This book contains the substance of a course of lectures recently given by the writer in the Queen Street Hall, Edinburgh. Its purpose is to indicate the Natural Principles governing the relation between Mental Action and Material Conditions...   New Age/Psychology Pages 148

☐ **Ayesha** *by H. Rider Haggard*   ISBN: *1-59462-301-5*   **$24.95**
Verily and indeed it is the unexpected that happens! Probably if there was one person upon the earth from whom the Editor of this, and of a certain previous history, did not expect to hear again...   Classics Pages 380

☐ **Ayala's Angel** *by Anthony Trollope*   ISBN: *1-59462-352-X*   **$29.95**
The two girls were both pretty, but Lucy who was twenty-one who supposed to be simple and comparatively unattractive, whereas Ayala was credited, as her Bombwhat romantic name might show, with poetic charm and a taste for romance. Ayala when her father died was nineteen...   Fiction Pages 484

☐ **The American Commonwealth** *by James Bryce*   ISBN: *1-59462-286-8*   **$34.45**
An interpretation of American democratic political theory. It examines political mechanics and society from the perspective of Scotsman James Bryce   Politics Pages 572

☐ **Stories of the Pilgrims** *by Margaret P. Pumphrey*   ISBN: *1-59462-116-0*   **$17.95**
This book explores pilgrims religious oppression in England as well as their escape to Holland and eventual crossing to America on the Mayflower, and their early days in New England...   History Pages 268

www.bookjungle.com *email: sales@bookjungle.com fax: 630-214-0564 mail: Book Jungle PO Box 2226 Champaign, IL 61825*

QTY

The Fasting Cure *by Sinclair Upton*   ISBN: *1-59462-222-1*   **$13.95**

In the Cosmopolitan Magazine for May, 1910, and in the Contemporary Review (London) for April, 1910, I published an article dealing with my experiences in fasting. I have written a great many magazine articles, but never one which attracted so much attention... New Age/Self Help/Health Pages 164

Hebrew Astrology *by Sepharial*   ISBN: *1-59462-308-2*   **$13.45**

In these days of advanced thinking it is a matter of common observation that we have left many of the old landmarks behind and that we are now pressing forward to greater heights and to a wider horizon than that which represented the mind-content of our progenitors... Astrology Pages 144

Thought Vibration or The Law of Attraction in the Thought World   ISBN: *1-59462-127-6*   **$12.95**

by William Walker Atkinson   *Psychology/Religion Pages 144*

Optimism *by Helen Keller*   ISBN: *1-59462-108-X*   **$15.95**

Helen Keller was blind, deaf, and mute since 19 months old, yet famously learned how to overcome these handicaps, communicate with the world, and spread her lectures promoting optimism. An inspiring read for everyone... Biographies/Inspirational Pages 84

Sara Crewe *by Frances Burnett*   ISBN: *1-59462-360-0*   **$9.45**

In the first place, Miss Minchin lived in London. Her home was a large, dull, tall one, in a large, dull square, where all the houses were alike, and all the sparrows were alike, and where all the door-knockers made the same heavy sound... Childrens/Classic Pages 88

The Autobiography of Benjamin Franklin *by Benjamin Franklin*   ISBN: *1-59462-135-7*   **$24.95**

The Autobiography of Benjamin Franklin has probably been more extensively read than any other American historical work, and no other book of its kind has had such ups and downs of fortune. Franklin lived for many years in England, where he was agent... Biographies/History Pages 332

Name	
Email	
Telephone	
Address	
City, State ZIP	

☐ **Credit Card**   ☐ **Check / Money Order**

Credit Card Number	
Expiration Date	
Signature	

Please Mail to: Book Jungle
PO Box 2226
Champaign, IL 61825
or Fax to: 630-214-0564

ORDERING INFORMATION

web: *www.bookjungle.com*
email: *sales@bookjungle.com*
fax: *630-214-0564*
mail: *Book Jungle PO Box 2226 Champaign, IL 61825*
or PayPal *to sales@bookjungle.com*

Please contact us for bulk discounts

DIRECT-ORDER TERMS

**20% Discount if You Order
Two or More Books**
Free Domestic Shipping!
Accepted: Master Card, Visa,
Discover, American Express